DEFIANCE

RESISTANCE
BOOK 2

New York

Published by First Second
First Second is an imprint of Roaring Brook Press,
a division of Holtzbrinck Publishing Holdings Limited Partnership,
175 Fifth Avenue, New York, NY 10010

Design by Colleen AF Venable

Colored by Hilary Sycamore and Sky Blue Ink. Lead colorist: Alex Campbell

Cataloging-in-Publication Data is on file at the Library of Congress.

ISBN: 978-1-59643-292-5

First Second books are available for special promotions and premiums.
For details, contact: Director of Special Markets, Holtzbrinck Publishers.

First Edition 2011
Printed in China by South China Printing Co. Ltd.,
Dongguan City, Guangdong Province
3 5 7 9 10 8 6 4 2

DEFIANCE

RESISTANCE BOOK 2

Written by
Carla Jablonski
Art by
Leland Purvis
Color by
Hilary Sycamore

First Second

ON JUNE 22, 1940, THE FRENCH AND THE GERMANS SIGNED AN ARMISTICE AGREEMENT. THE FRENCH WOULD STOP FIGHTING AND AGREE TO GERMAN DEMANDS. NOT EVEN A YEAR HAD PASSED SINCE FRANCE AND BRITAIN DECLARED WAR ON THE NAZIS. BUT FRANCE COULDN'T WIN AGAINST THE GERMAN ARMY.

NOW, THREE YEARS INTO THE OCCUPATION, THE FRENCH HAVE BEEN LIVING WITH SHORTAGES OF ALL KINDS, DISAPPEARANCES, DENUNCIATIONS, AND FEAR. THOUSANDS HAVE BEEN FORCED FROM THEIR HOMES; MANY ARE IN HIDING. ALMOST TWO MILLION FRENCH MEN—FATHERS, HUSBANDS, SONS, AND FRIENDS—ARE STILL PRISONERS OF WAR. MANY MORE HAVE BEEN ARRESTED AND DEPORTED—OR EXECUTED FOR RESISTING. RESISTING THE NEW LAWS, RULES, AND LIMITATIONS IMPOSED BY THE OCCUPIERS.

BUT IT ISN'T ONLY THE GERMAN MILITARY ENFORCING THE RULES OR CREATING HARDSHIPS. NEIGHBORS INFORM ON NEIGHBORS; MANY TAKE ADVANTAGE OF THE SHORTAGES TO DEMAND HIGH PRICES OR SELL ON THE BLACK MARKET; OTHERS COLLABORATE WITH THE GERMANS, WELCOMING THEM INTO THEIR BUSINESSES AND THEIR LIVES. AS THE OCCUPATION CONTINUES, THE SEEMINGLY ENDLESS WAR MAKES TENSIONS RISE TO THE SURFACE—AND THE FRENCH OFTEN TURN AGAINST THE FRENCH.

IN 1943, TO ENSURE THEIR CONTINUED CONTROL, THE GERMANS CREATE A NEW AND VICIOUS POLICE FORCE: THE MILICE (FRENCH MILITARY POLICE). THE GERMANS HAVE NO TROUBLE FILLING THE RANKS WITH EAGER FRENCH VOLUNTEERS. AND TO KEEP THE WAR MACHINE RUNNING, THE GERMANS INSTITUTE COMPULSORY LABOR PROGRAMS, SENDING YOUNG MEN AND WOMEN TO GERMANY TO WORK FOR THE GERMAN WAR EFFORT.

THESE TWO NEW ADDITIONS TO THE GERMAN STRATEGY, SUPPORTED BY VICHY, RESULT IN A RISE IN NEW FORMS OF RESISTANCE...

Noch einen!
Ist unmöglich, blödsinnig !!

PAUL!
HAVE ANY RATION TICKETS TO TRADE?
I HAVE SOME TOBACCO TICKETS.
WHERE DID YOU GET THEM?
I HAVE MY SECRETS.

HE STOLE THEM!
ARE YOU GOING TO TELL YOUR FATHER? MISTER BIG SHOT POLICEMAN?

!?
!!
WHAT ARE THE BOCHES BOTHERING ABOUT NOW?

THOSE HORRID PICTURES!

YOU DON'T LIKE THEM?
THEY'RE SO UGLY!

I LIKE THEM!

TAKE THAT, YOU FILTHY BOCHE!
QUIT IT!

MY FATHER SAYS THE PICTURES ARE DANGEROUS.

HOW SO?

HE SAYS IT ISN'T A GOOD IDEA TO MAKE THE GERMANS ANGRY.

Ach. Ist ganz gefehr-lich!
Das geht nich' hier!!

HEY, WHAT'S GOING ON?
DON'T ATTRACT THEIR ATTENTION!
THE VANDALS ARE AT IT AGAIN.
THEY'RE GOING TO GET THEMSELVES KILLED.
KILLED?
THE GERMANS TAKE THEMSELVES VERY SERIOUSLY.
TO MOCK THEM THIS WAY IS A CRIME AGAINST THE STATE.
THE GERMAN STATE? I THOUGHT WE WERE STILL FRENCH.
THAT'S RIGHT!
WE WERE A REPUBLIC. NOW WE'RE A STATE.

TAKE CARE. YOU MAY BE YOUNG, BUT DISRESPECT WILL NOT BE TOLERATED.
AND THESE POSTERS ARE TREASONOUS.
THEY RIDICULE THE FRENCH POLICE AS MUCH AS THE GERMANS.
THAT'S BECAUSE-
I SHOULD GO.
MY MOTHER IS WAITING.

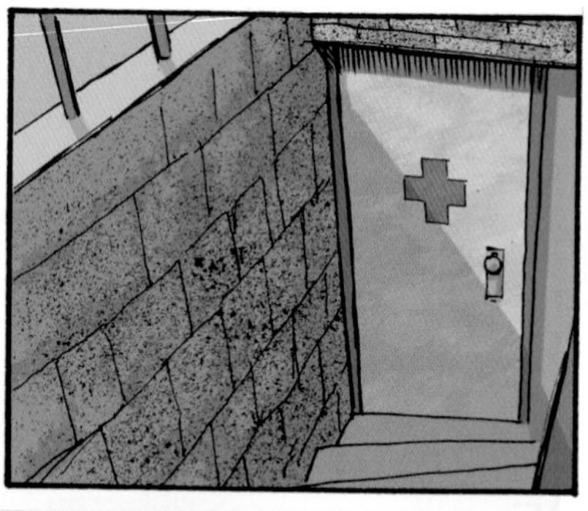

WHY WON'T THEY SEND US WHAT WE NEED?
THEY ARE STRETCHED TO THEIR LIMITS.
YOU KNOW THAT'S NOT THE REAL REASON! THEY DON'T WANT TO ARM ANYONE BUT THE MEN PUT IN PLACE BY DEGAULLE.
WE TAKE OUR ORDERS FROM GENERAL DEGAULLE. THE FREE FRENCH HAVE BEEN WORKING VERY HARD TO UNITE THE GROUPS SO THAT WE WILL BE EFFECTIVE, NOT JUST RABBLE-ROUSING HOTHEADS.
LIKE **ME**, YOU MEAN.

DEGAULLE HAS A POINT.
HE HAS PROTOCOL. HE LIKES TITLES AND RANKS AND THINGS NICE AND TIDY. WHAT CAN HE DO FROM LONDON?
TO LIBERATE FRANCE WE MUST BECOME AN ARMY.
A TRUE MILITARY OPERATION.
HOW CAN WE DO THAT WITHOUT WEAPONS?
TRUTH IS ALSO A WEAPON. NOW GO DISTRIBUTE THESE PAPERS. WE MUST COUNTER THE VICHY PROPAGANDA. KEEP MORALE UP. CREATE A GREATER RESOLVE IN OUR PEOPLE TO—
TO DO NOTHING. TO READ SOME PAMPHLETS. FORGET IT. A CHILD COULD DO THAT WORK.
EVEN A CHILD WILL BE SHOT IF FOUND DISTRIBUTING THESE, AND IF NOT THE CHILD, THEN THE FAMILY. YOU KNOW THAT.

WE'RE WASTING TIME.
WE NEED TO TAKE ACTION BEFORE THE FOOD SHORTAGES GET WORSE AND WE'RE ALL TOO WEAK TO DO ANYTHING.

VIOLENCE ISN'T THE ONLY WAY.
MAYBE NOT.
BUT IT'S VERY EFFECTIVE.

I SEE YOU'VE PICKED UP YOUR LITTLE SISTER'S HABIT OF EAVESDROPPING.

HERE'S YOUR CHILD FOR YOUR BABY'S TASK. NOW I'M OFF TO DO A MAN'S WORK.

WHY IS JACQUES SO MAD?

HE'S JUST FRUSTRATED.

AND THAT'S A GOOD WAY TO GET PEOPLE KILLED.

Salon de Coiffure
THE DOG KNOCKED OVER THE GARBAGE BIN AGAIN.
CAN YOU FIX IT? I'LL BE RIGHT OUT TO HELP YOU.
Salon de Coiffu
SURE THING.

YOU'RE NOT THE USUAL CONTACT.
I'M THE ONE TODAY. I DON'T KNOW IF IT WILL BE ME NEXT WEEK.
YOU'RE MADAME TESSIER'S BOY.
YOU GO TO SCHOOL WITH MY NEPHEW, BERNARD CHAPPUIS.
CLOSED MOUTHED. VERY SMART.

MUST BE HAVING TROUBLE GETTING PAPER, THERE ARE FEWER THIS TIME.
I GUESS...

TAKE GOOD CARE.
I ALWAYS DO.

I HOPE THAT'S TRUE.

Tessier
Vinicole

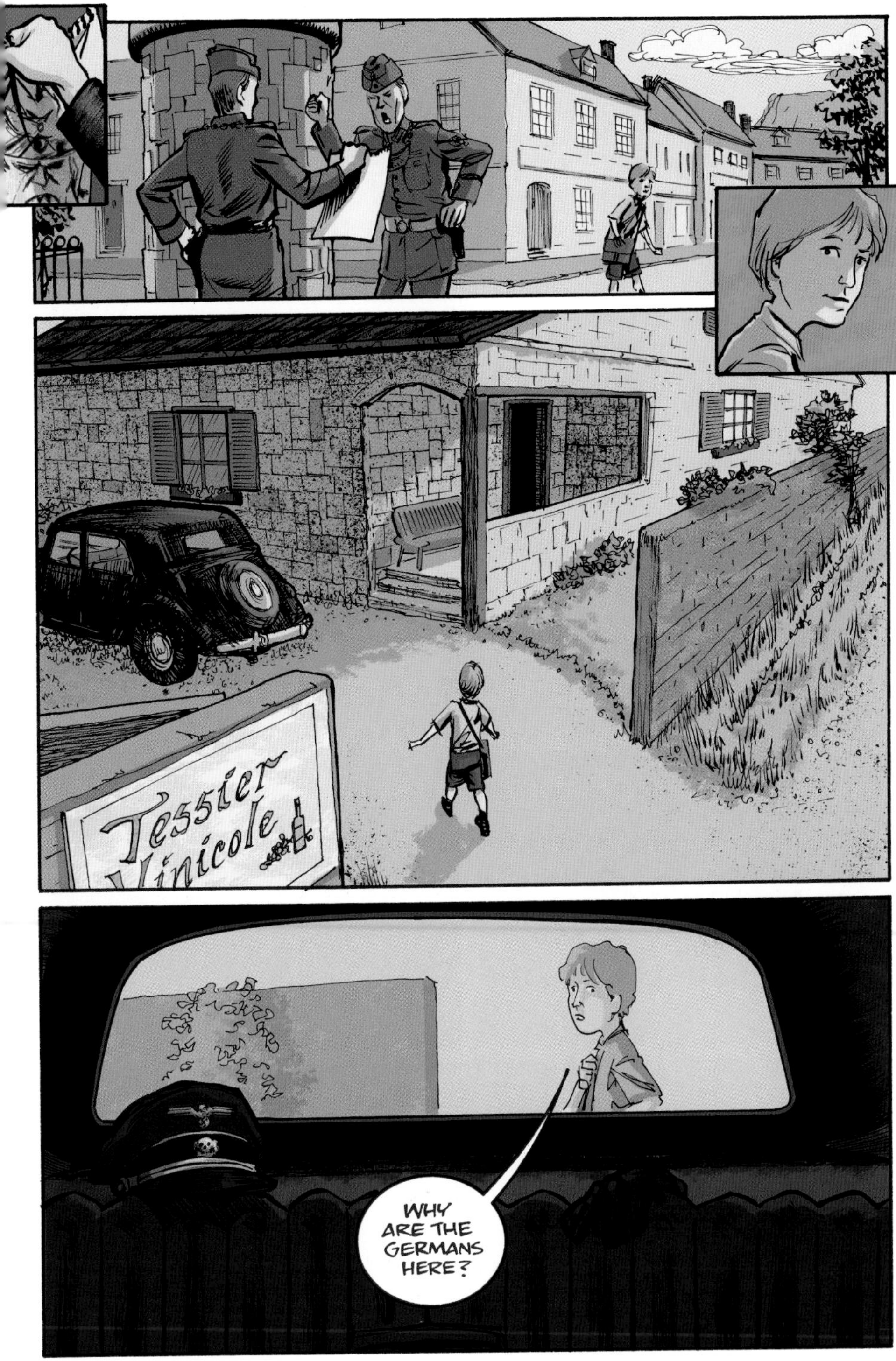

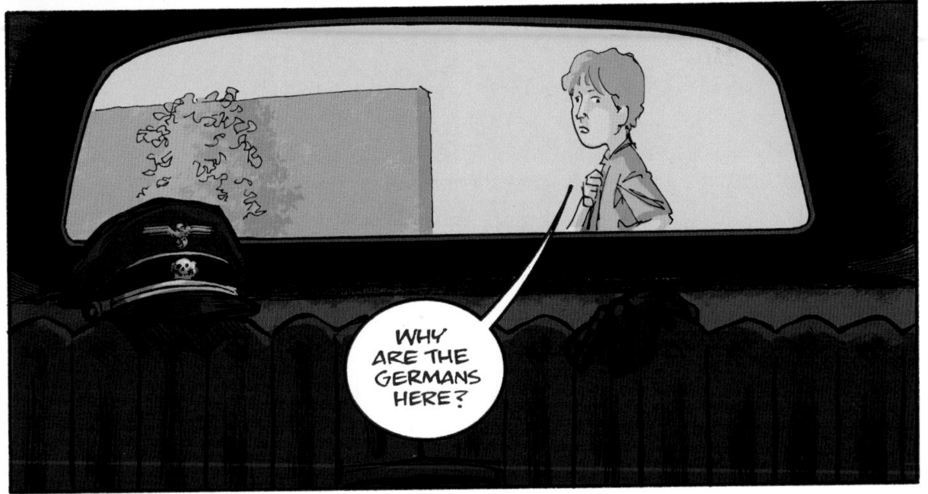
WHY ARE THE GERMANS HERE?

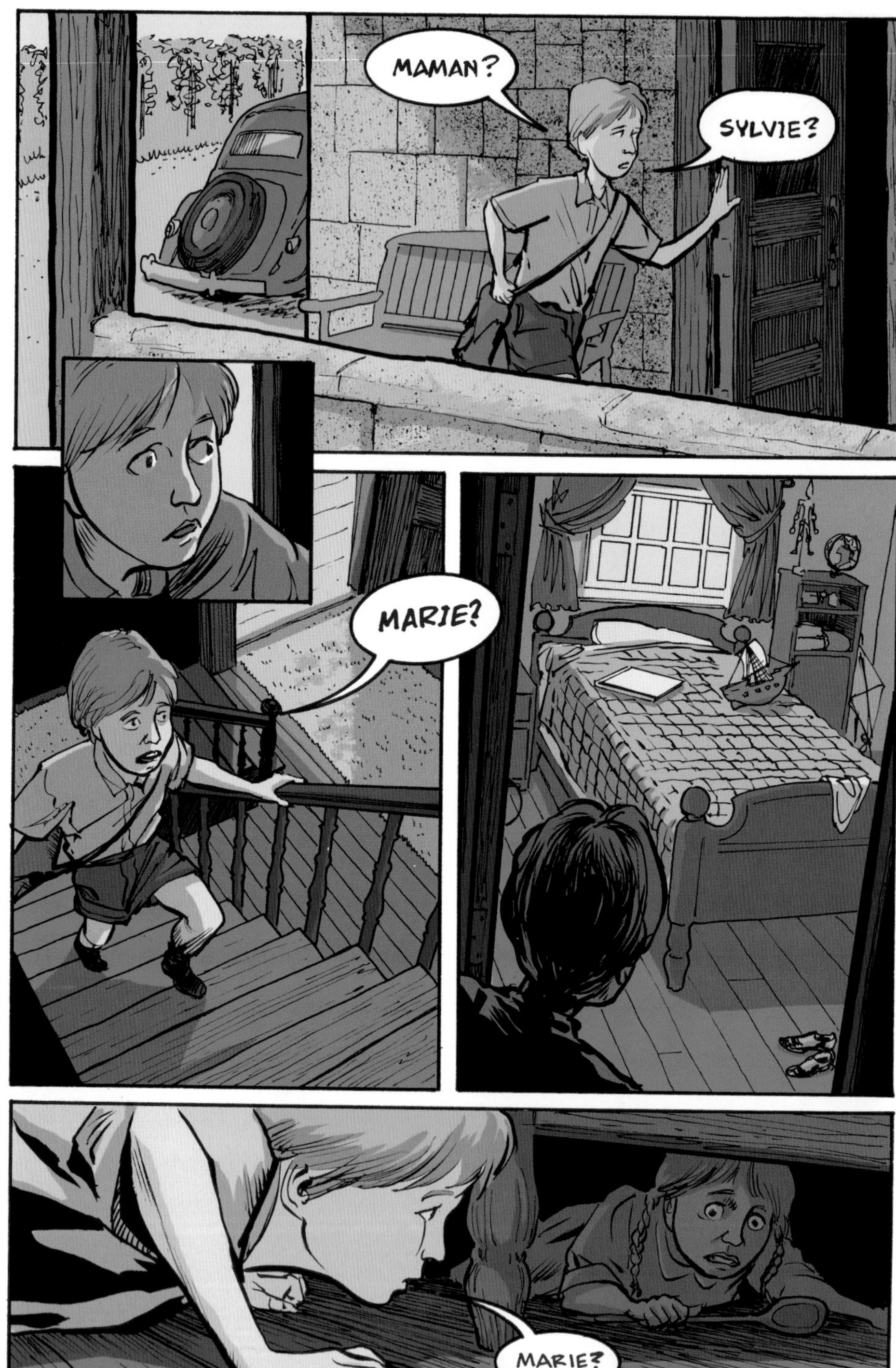
MAMAN?
SYLVIE?
MARIE?
MARIE?

WHAT'S GOING ON?
WHERE'S MAMAN?
I DON'T KNOW.

DID THE GERMANS TAKE HER?
I DON'T KNOW.

DON'T YOU KNOW ANYTHING?

I SAW THE CAR AND THE GERMANS, SO I HID UNDER THE BED.

VENEZ À MOI AVEC CONFIANCE
STAY HERE. I'LL GO FIND OUT.

WE'LL EXPECT AN ADDITIONAL 200 LITERS FROM YOU.
WE'RE ALREADY SELLING TO YOU BELOW OUR COSTS!
THIS ISN'T TO DRINK, MADAME. WE'LL TURN THIS ALCOHOL INTO FUEL FOR OUR CARS.
BUT WHAT ARE WE TO LIVE ON? THE WINE IS HOW WE—
SOMEONE WILL BE OUT TOMORROW WITH DRUMS TO TRANSPORT IT IN, AND TO BE SURE YOU DON'T TRY TO SELL IT OUT FROM UNDER US...
NO ONE WILL DRINK THIS NOW.

OH, DIDIER. IF ONLY YOU WERE HERE. YOU WOULD KNOW HOW TO STAND UP TO THEM.

MAMAN, IT'S OKAY!
PLEASE DON'T CRY.

PAUL! I DIDN'T HEAR YOU.

WHAT DID THOSE GERMANS WANT?
WHAT'S OURS. AS USUAL.
CAN THEY REALLY TAKE OUR WINE?

THEY ARE THE OCCUPIERS. THEY CAN TAKE WHAT THEY WANT. I SUPPOSE WE'RE LUCKY. THEY COULD HAVE TAKEN EVERYTHING. BUT...
...THE CASKS!
THEY'VE BEEN PART OF OUR WINERY FOR GENERATIONS. AND NOW—THEY'RE RUINED.
BUT HE SAID THAT THEY WEREN'T GOING TO TAKE THE CASKS.
THEY'RE BRINGING THEIR OWN—
NO.
HE THOUGHT HE WAS SIMPLY SPOILING THE WINE. THAT'S BAD ENOUGH. BUT THE CASKS! THAT HEATING OIL HE POURED IN. IT DESTROYS THE WOOD. NOTHING WILL BRING IT BACK.
I COULD KILL EVERY GERMAN I SEE.
DON'T TALK OF KILLING.
THERE'S BEEN ENOUGH VIOLENCE.
COME. LET'S CHECK ON MARIE. SHE MUST BE FRIGHTENED.

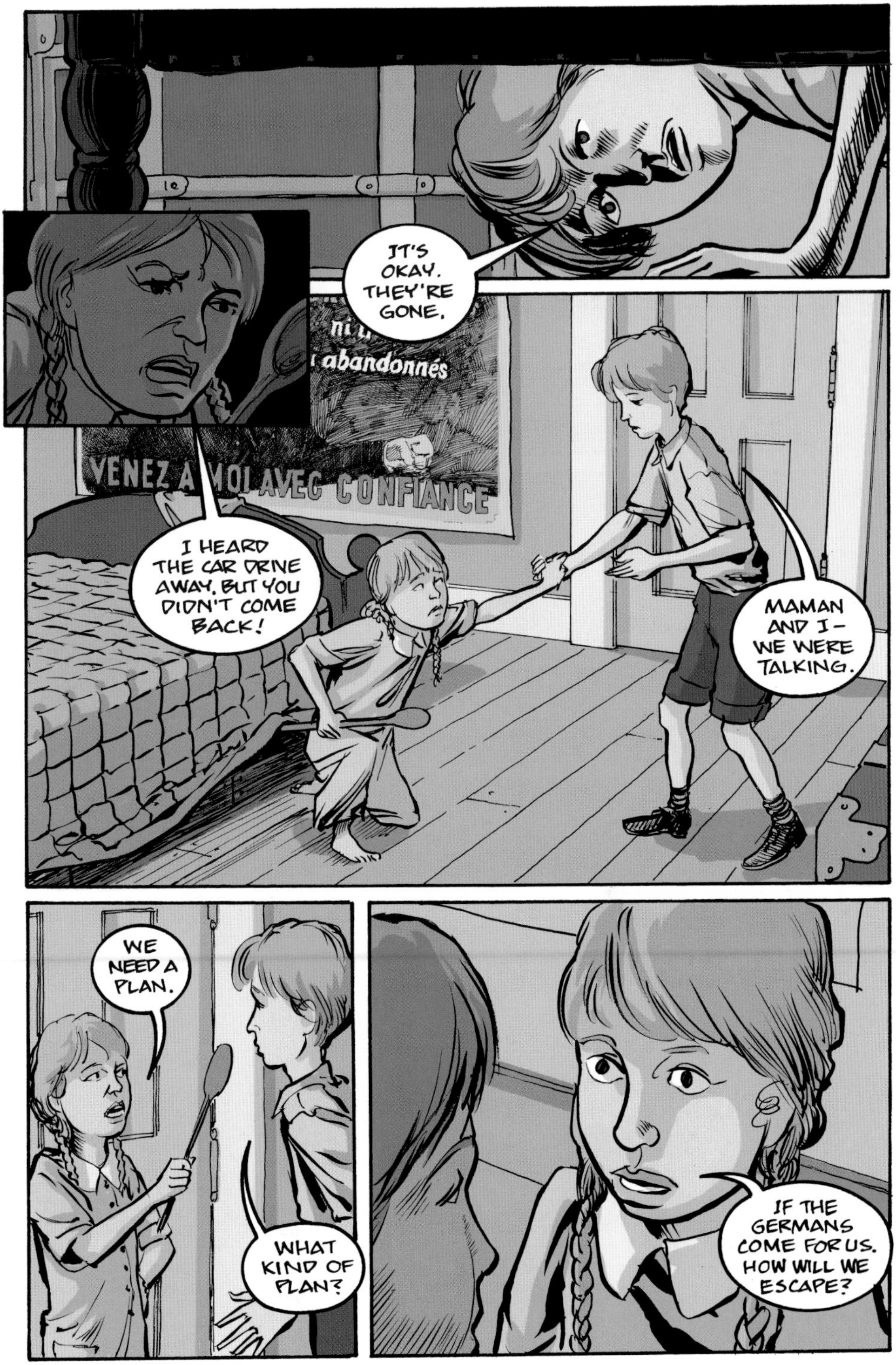

IT'S OKAY. THEY'RE GONE.

I HEARD THE CAR DRIVE AWAY. BUT YOU DIDN'T COME BACK!

abandonnés

VENEZ A MOI AVEC CONFIANCE

MAMAN AND I— WE WERE TALKING.

WE NEED A PLAN.
WHAT KIND OF PLAN?
IF THE GERMANS COME FOR US. HOW WILL WE ESCAPE?

AS LONG AS WE'RE CAREFUL—
MR. AND MRS. LEVY WERE CAREFUL! THEY TOOK THEM AWAY!
THAT WAS DIFFERENT. THEY TOOK THEM BECAUSE THEY WERE JEWISH.
vous n'ête
abandonnés
VENEZ A M
THEY'RE ONLY ALIVE BECAUSE THEY ESCAPED. AND HENRI WOULD NEVER HAVE MADE IT TO HIS PARENTS WITHOUT OUR HELP. BUT WHO WILL HELP US?
WE'LL HELP EACH OTHER.
BUT WHAT WILL I DO IF YOU... WHAT IF I... HOW WILL I...
WE JUST HAVE TO BE SURE IT DOESN'T HAPPEN.

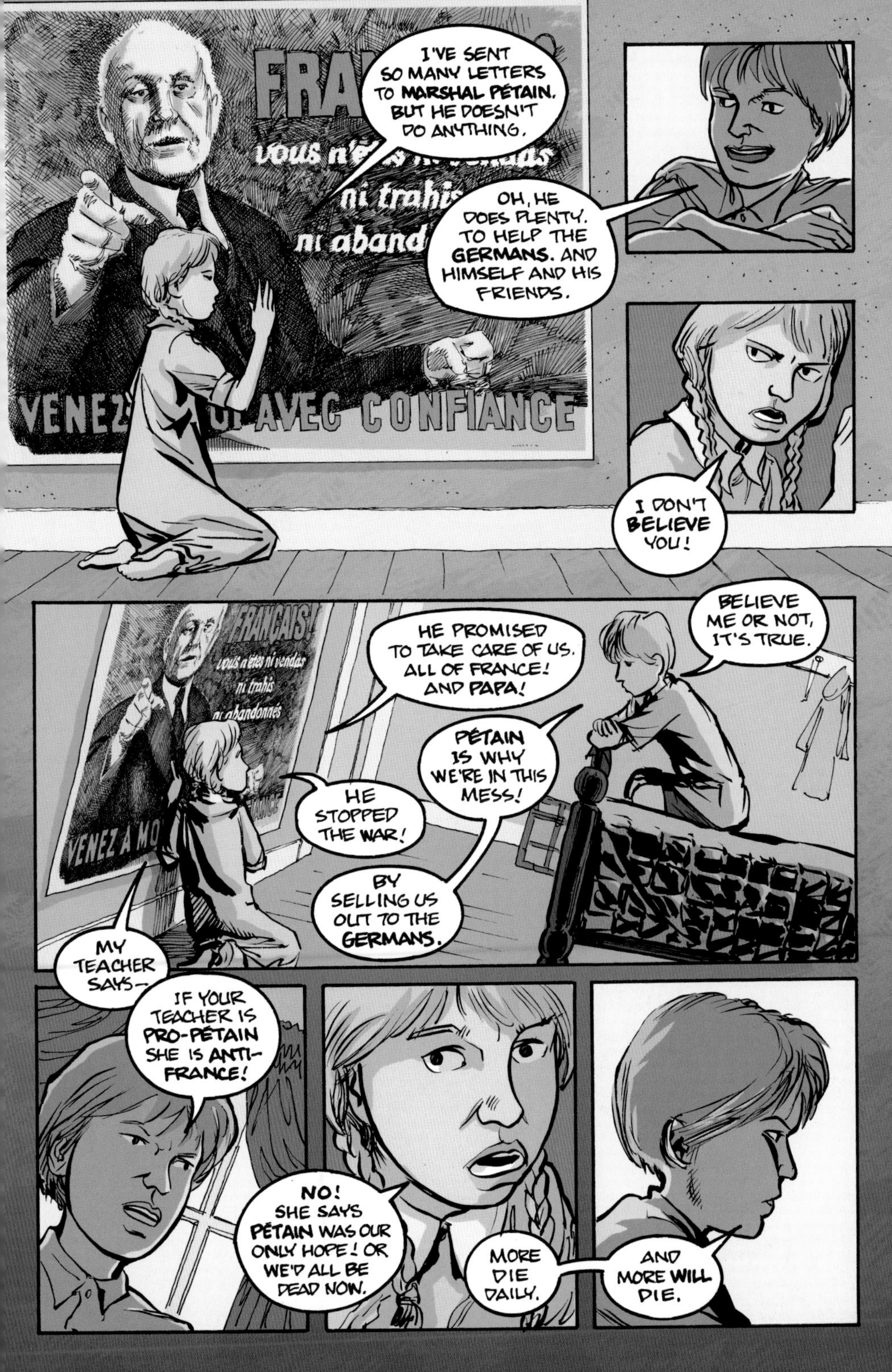
I'VE SENT SO MANY LETTERS TO **MARSHAL PÉTAIN**. BUT HE DOESN'T DO ANYTHING.
VENEZ AVEC CONFIANCE
OH, HE DOES PLENTY. TO HELP THE **GERMANS**. AND HIMSELF AND HIS FRIENDS.
I DON'T **BELIEVE** YOU!
FRANÇAIS!
vous n'êtes ni vendus
ni trahis
ni abandonnés
VENEZ A MO
BELIEVE ME OR NOT, IT'S TRUE.
HE PROMISED TO TAKE CARE OF US. ALL OF FRANCE! AND **PAPA**!
PÉTAIN IS WHY WE'RE IN THIS MESS!
HE STOPPED THE **WAR**!
BY SELLING US OUT TO THE **GERMANS**.
MY TEACHER SAYS—
IF YOUR TEACHER IS **PRO-PÉTAIN** SHE IS **ANTI-FRANCE**!
NO! SHE SAYS **PÉTAIN** WAS OUR ONLY HOPE! OR WE'D ALL BE DEAD NOW.
MORE DIE DAILY.
AND MORE **WILL** DIE.

MARSHAL PÉTAIN! HERE WE ARE! WE STAND BEFORE YOU!
IF YOU ARE FOR PÉTAIN, YOU ARE AGAINST ME. AND JACQUES.
VEC CONFIANCE
THE SAVIOR OF FRANCE WE VOW TO YOU AND ALL
AGAINST ALL THOSE WHO HELP PEOPLE LIKE HENRI AND MR AND MRS. LEVY.
I'M NOT!
AUNT CELIA! I THOUGHT YOU HAD ALREADY LEFT.
WHAT'S GOING ON IN HERE?
NOTHING. RIGHT, MARIE?
MARIE, ARE YOU CRYING?

PAUL SAYS I CAN'T DRAW.
BUT I TOLD HIM I DON'T CARE. BECAUSE I DO BETTER IN ALL MY OTHER SUBJECTS THAN HE WILL ANY DAY.
PAUL, DON'T YOU HAVE ANYTHING BETTER TO DO THAN BOTHER YOUR LITTLE SISTER?
VENE
YOU'RE OLD ENOUGH TO BE OF SOME HELP AROUND HERE. YOU SHOULD BE TAKING YOUR FATHER'S PLACE.
DON'T SAY THAT! PAPA WILL BE HOME SOON!
I ONLY MEANT...
JUST SEE IF YOUR MOTHER NEEDS ANYTHING. BOTH OF YOU. I'M GOING OUT.

WE HAVE TO BE MORE CAREFUL WITH AUNT CELIA IN THE HOUSE.

I'M GOING TO CHECK IF MAMAN NEEDS HELP WITH DINNER, NOT THAT THERE'S GOING TO BE MUCH TO IT.
YOU COMING?
IN A MINUTE.

YOU LIED.

I THOUGHT YOU LIKED ME. YOU JUST WANT ME TO WORK FOR YOUR STUPID CAUSE!
YOU KNOW THAT'S NOT TRUE.
I DON'T KNOW WHAT TO THINK ANYMORE.

THIS ASSIGNMENT IS PERFECT FOR YOU. YOU'RE SO PRETTY. YOU JUST HAVE TO DO WHAT YOU DO BEST. HAVE FUN, BUT I'LL GIVE YOU SOME QUESTIONS TO ASK.
IF I GO WITH GERMAN BOYS MY FRIENDS WILL HATE ME!

NOT ALL OF THEM. MANY OF THEM GO ON DATES WITH THEM.

YOU'VE DONE IT YOURSELF.
NOW I JUST WANT YOU TO FIND OUT SOME INFORMATION WHEN YOU DO.

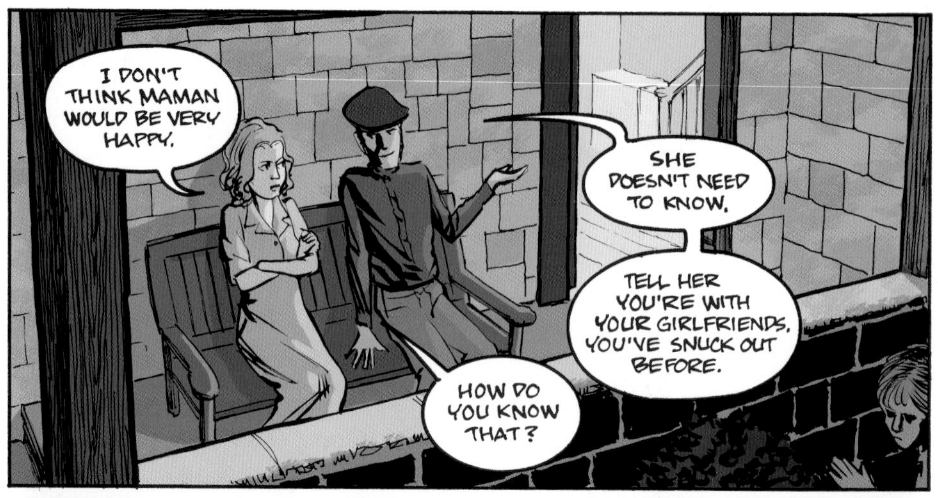
I DON'T THINK MAMAN WOULD BE VERY HAPPY.
SHE DOESN'T NEED TO KNOW.
TELL HER YOU'RE WITH YOUR GIRLFRIENDS. YOU'VE SNUCK OUT BEFORE.
HOW DO YOU KNOW THAT?

YOU CERTAINLY HAVE BEEN PAYING ATTENTION TO MY ACTIVITIES, HAVEN'T YOU?
YOU INTEREST ME.

WHAT DO YOU WANT HER TO FIND OUT?

YOUNG TESSIER, CONVINCE YOUR SISTER.
YOU SHOULD BE MORE CAREFUL.
I JUST SNUCK UP ON YOU. HEARD EVERY WORD.

THE LATEST ART SHOW- YOUR WORK, I'M GUESSING?

YOU PROMISED MAMAN THAT AFTER WE BROUGHT HENRI TO PARIS YOU'D STOP. NO MORE RESISTANCE WORK!

I DID STOP. FOR A WHILE.
AND THINGS HAVE GOTTEN EVEN WORSE. OR HAVE YOU BEEN TOO BUSY SNEAKING OUT TO PARTIES TO NOTICE?
OH, SHUT UP!

YOU SEE? I'M NOT ASKING YOU TO DO ANYTHING YOU AREN'T ALREADY DOING!
NO. I'M TIRED OF SECRETS. OF LIES.
DOES THAT MEAN YOU'RE GOING TO STOP SNEAKING OUT AT NIGHT?
WHAT I DO IS NONE OF YOUR BUSINESS.
YOURS EITHER.
YOU DON'T CARE ABOUT ME AT ALL. YOU JUST WANT TO USE ME FOR YOUR OWN PLANS.
I'M SICK OF IT.

SHE'LL GET OVER IT. SHE'S ALWAYS THROWING SOME KIND OF FIT.
GIRLS CAN BE DANGEROUS WHEN THEY'RE ANGRY. I'LL HAVE TO KEEP AN EYE ON HER. I'D HATE IT IF—

WHAT ARE YOU SAYING?
JUST THAT A HAPPY SYLVIE IS A HANDFUL.
ONE IN A MOOD... WELL...

TOO TRUE.
AUNT CELIA OFF WITH HER BLACK-MARKET SUITOR?

I HATE THOSE SHINY DRESSES HE GIVES HER. MAMAN LOOKS SO DRAB BESIDE HER.
SHE DOESN'T GET ANYTHING FOR YOUR FAMILY?
MAMAN WON'T LET HER. I HEARD THEM ARGUING ABOUT IT.
THERE ARE OTHER WAYS TO MAKE ACQUISITIONS.
WHAT DID YOU WANT SYLVIE TO DO?
THERE ARE GROUPS—RESISTANTS—WHO HAVE TAKEN TO THE WOODS. THEY LIVE IN THE PROTECTION OF THE JURA MOUNTAINS. THEY ARE TRAINING, HIDING, FIGHTING.
LIKE OUTLAWS?
NOT QUITE SO ROMANTIC AS THAT.

WHO ARE THEY?
ALL TYPES.
PEOPLE YOU MIGHT EXPECT, AND PEOPLE YOU'D NEVER IMAGINE. THEY MEAN TO TAKE ACTION—ONCE THEY ARE BETTER ARMED.
THEY'RE KNOWN AS THE **MAQUIS.**

HOW DOES **SYLVIE** FIGURE INTO THIS?

WE'RE TRYING TO FIND OUT HOW MUCH THE GERMANS KNOW ABOUT THE MAQUIS. IF THEY KNOW THEIR LOCATIONS.

AND YOU WANTED SYLVIE TO TALK TO THE GERMANS NEXT DOOR?

THEY'RE YOUNGER, THEY'RE BORED. AND AS MUCH AS SHE ANNOYS YOU, OTHERS FIND HER... CHARMING.
HARD TO BELIEVE.

WE'LL JUST HAVE TO GET OUR INFORMATION ANOTHER WAY, AND MAKE SURE **SYLVIE** DOESN'T REVEAL OUR PURPOSE.
SHE WON'T.

I'M SURE.

WE'LL SEE...
AND THEN WE'LL SEE WHAT WE NEED TO DO.

GET AWAY FROM HERE!
YOU ALREADY TOOK HIS FATHER!

KEEP YOUR EYES ON YOUR WORK. WHATEVER IS HAPPENING OUTSIDE IS NOT OUR AFFAIR.
HOW CAN YOU DO THIS? AND TO YOUR OWN COUNTRYMEN!
YOU WILL ROT IN HELL!

WHAT'S HAPPENING?
ARE THEY ARRESTING SOMEONE?
I'M NOT SURE.
I KNOW YOUR FAMILIES! DO YOU THINK YOUR MOTHERS ARE PROUD?
PTUI
SLAM
KLAC

FRANCE
1943
PÉTAIN
ALL RIGHT. SHOW'S OVER. BACK TO WORK.
WE'LL ASK **LUCIE**. HER FATHER IS A POLICEMAN. SHE'LL KNOW WHAT'S GOING ON.
HE'S REGULAR POLICE. THESE ARE THE FRENCH MILITIA. THAT'S DIFFERENT.
SHE'LL KNOW.

OF COURSE, IT'S TERRIBLE. BUT WHAT CAN ANYONE DO?
I WOULDN'T GO! I'D RUN AWAY!

MY FATHER SAYS THAT'S EXACTLY WHAT'S GOING TO HAPPEN.
WHAT WERE THE MILITARY POLICEMEN DOING?
HAVEN'T YOU HEARD?
THE FRENCH ARE NOW MOVING TO GERMANY. WHETHER THEY WANT TO OR NOT!

WHAT DO YOU MEAN?

THEY'RE TAKING MEN TO GERMANY TO WORK IN THE FACTORIES THERE.

NOW THE FRENCH ARE EXPECTED TO HELP THE GERMANS KILL US?

IT'S NOT LIKE THAT. **MARSHAL PÉTAIN** WOULDN'T MAKE FRENCHMEN KILL THEIR OWN PEOPLE! THAT'S STUPID.
WE DON'T KNOW WHAT HE DOES. OR WILL DO.
IT'S JUST WHILE THE WAR IS ON. AND THIS WAY THEY CAN MAKE MONEY!
THAT'S TRUE! IT WOULD BE NICE TO BE ABLE TO BUY THINGS AGAIN.
LIKE **FOOD!**
FOOD.
I DON'T THINK IT'S GOING TO WORK LIKE THAT.
MY FATHER SAID THEY'RE SUPPOSED TO DO IT AS AN EXCHANGE-FOR PRISONERS OF WAR.
THEY'VE SAID THAT BEFORE. IT NEVER HAPPENS.
NEVER?

WHEN ARE YOU GOING TO RESCUE MY PAPA?

DO YOU HEAR ME? NEVER!
LET GO OF MY ARM.

NOT UNTIL I KNOW YOU UNDERSTAND ME.
OW!

LEAVE HER ALONE!
SHE IS OLD ENOUGH TO UNDERSTAND.

YOU PUT US ALL IN DANGER WITH YOUR LOOSE TONGUE. THAT IS **UNFORGIVABLE.**
HEY—
FINE! I UNDERSTAND. SORRY.

YOU MAKE MISTAKES, TOO. YOU TALK WHERE PEOPLE CAN HEAR YOU.

I'VE TOLD YOU, MARIE. I CAN'T.
YOU HELP OTHER PEOPLE ESCAPE.
PEOPLE IN HIDING. PEOPLE WHO HAVE BEEN ARRESTED.
MY FATHER IS IN PRISON!
HE'S A PRISONER OF WAR. THAT'S DIFFERENT.
IT'S ALMOST MY BIRTHDAY!
AND PAPA WILL MISS IT.
AGAIN.
I HOPE I HAVEN'T MADE A MISTAKE, TRUSTING YOU AND YOUR FAMILY— YOUR SISTERS.
IT WILL BE FINE.

ARE YOU DOING HOMEWORK?
I'M MAKING A PLAN. YOU'LL SEE. WE'LL RESCUE **PAPA**.
IT'S NOT AS TERRIBLE FOR PAPA IN THE **P.O.W.** CAMP. IT'S WORSE FOR THE ONES WHO ARE CAUGHT DOING RESISTANCE WORK. THOSE ARE THE ONES **JACQUES** HAS TO HELP ESCAPE.
DO YOU THINK **HENRI** WILL SEND ME A BIRTHDAY CARD?
HE MIGHT NOT REMEMBER WHEN IT IS.
PAPA WILL. HE DID LAST YEAR, REMEMBER?
HE DREW ME A PICTURE. JUST LIKE YOU DID.

HAVE YOU TOLD ANYONE ABOUT OUR SECRET WAR?
OF COURSE NOT.
HAVE YOU?
I'M NOT STUPID!
IT'S PAPA. AND ME!
SO NO MATTER WHAT, HE'LL BE HERE FOR YOUR BIRTHDAY.

NOW WHAT'S WRONG?
THEY TOOK JACQUES!
ARRESTED?
NO, THANK GOODNESS.
IT'S JUST THE WORK PROGRAM. SYLVIE IS MAKING TOO MUCH OF IT.
THE FORCED LABOR, YOU MEAN. AGAINST OUR WILL.
HUSH, CHILD. YOU'RE NOT OLD ENOUGH TO UNDERSTAND SUCH THINGS.
YOU'RE THE ONE WHO DOESN'T UNDERSTAND. YOU—
PAUL! ENOUGH!

I'M GLAD WE WON'T BE SEEING HIM AROUND ANYMORE.

HE'S A TERRIBLE INFLUENCE.

YOU'VE BEEN SPENDING FAR TOO MUCH TIME WITH HIM.

DON'T YOU TWO HAVE HOMEWORK TO DO?

WELL? GO DO IT!

WITH YOUR FATHER GONE, YOUR MOTHER HAS TOO MUCH ON HER PLATE TO KEEP YOU CHILDREN IN LINE. SOMEONE HAS TO MAINTAIN DISCIPLINE.

YOU SHOULD HAVE INSISTED SHE COME DOWN TO DINNER.
SHE'S UPSET. LET HER CRY IT OUT.
YOUR CHILDREN HAVE BECOME QUITE IMPERTINENT. YOU AREN'T MAINTAINING PROPER AUTHORITY. WHAT WOULD **DIDIER** THINK?

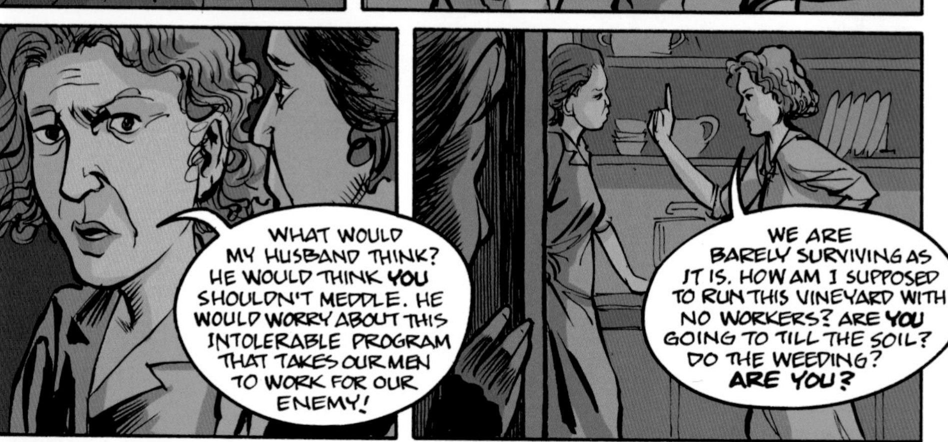
WHAT WOULD MY HUSBAND THINK? HE WOULD THINK **YOU** SHOULDN'T MEDDLE. HE WOULD WORRY ABOUT THIS INTOLERABLE PROGRAM THAT TAKES OUR MEN TO WORK FOR OUR ENEMY!
WE ARE BARELY SURVIVING AS IT IS. HOW AM I SUPPOSED TO RUN THIS VINEYARD WITH NO WORKERS? ARE **YOU** GOING TO TILL THE SOIL? DO THE WEEDING? **ARE YOU?**

WE TOOK YOU IN. WE PUT A ROOF OVER YOUR HEAD AND FED YOU— WITH OUR OWN RATION COUPONS! AND YOU STAND THERE AND SPOUT HOW **PÉTAIN** IS—

YOUR HUSBAND IS ALIVE!
IF **MARSHAL PÉTAIN** HADN'T AGREED TO THE ARMISTICE, YOUR **DIDIER** MIGHT HAVE BEEN ANOTHER CASUALTY!

THE GERMANS ARE GOING TO **WIN** THIS WAR. AND WHEN THEY DO, WHICH SIDE DO YOU WANT TO HAVE BEEN ON?

KNOCK KNOCK

CAN I COME IN?

IS EVERYONE ASLEEP?

MAMAN IS PACING IN HER ROOM. AGAIN. I DON'T THINK SHE EVER SLEEPS ANYMORE.

DID JACQUES TELL YOU WHAT HE WANTED ME TO DO?

WHY?
WHAT IF SOMETHING HAPPENS TO HIM? WHAT IF I COULD HAVE HELPED HIM AND I DIDN'T?
IT'S A HUGE SECRET. WILL YOU BE ABLE TO KEEP IT?
OF COURSE!
I'VE KEPT PLENTY ALREADY, REMEMBER?
IS IT... IS IT HARD FOR YOU TO LIE SO MUCH?
WHAT'S THAT SUPPOSED TO MEAN?
IT'S JUST THAT I—I FIND IT SO **EASY**.
IS THAT BAD?
I GUESS THAT DEPENDS ON WHAT YOU'RE LYING ABOUT.

JACQUES WANTED YOU TO FIND OUT IF THE GERMANS KNOW ANYTHING ABOUT THE RESISTANCE GROUPS HIDING IN THE MOUNTAINS.
THE MAQUIS?
DANCES AND DRESSES AREN'T ALL I KNOW.
WILL YOU FIND OUT?
BUT IF I GET THE INFORMATION, WHO DO I GIVE IT TO? JACQUES IS GONE!
LEAVE IT TO ME.

PAUL, GO FIND MARIE. SHE'S OUTSIDE SOMEWHERE.
BUT-
JUST DO IT.
CHECK THE VINEYARD. SHE'S NOT IN THE YARD.
OKAY.
WITH ALL THAT'S GOING ON DO I ALSO HAVE TO WORRY ABOUT WHERE YOU THREE ARE?

WHAT ARE YOU DOING?
MAMAN IS GOING TO LOSE THE WINERY WITHOUT WORKERS. SO I'M HELPING.
I ONLY KNOW ABOUT WEEDING. PAPA NEVER SHOWED ME ANYTHING ELSE.
HE NEVER SHOWED ME ANYTHING EITHER. I ASKED BEFORE HE LEFT, BUT HE SAID I WAS TOO SMALL.
WE HAVE TO FIND OUT. THERE'S NO ONE BIGGER THAN US ANY-MORE.

DON'T LET THE GERMANS
TURN THE FRENCH
AGAINST THE FRENCH!

DEGAULLE'S SYMBOL!

ANOTHER RÉSISTANT!

PAUL TESSIER! YOU'RE UP EARLY.
FORGET THAT THERE WAS NO SCHOOL TODAY?
GOOD MORNING, **MONSIEUR ROGET.** HI, LUCIE.
HI, PAUL.

PAUL, DON'T BE SO NERVOUS! JUST BECAUSE I'M A POLICEMAN DOESN'T MEAN I GO AROUND ARRESTING EVERYBODY.
DON'T WORRY, PULLING A GIRL'S PIGTAILS WON'T LAND YOU IN JAIL, SON.
RIGHT. I'LL REMEMBER THAT. I—I REALLY NEED TO—

OF COURSE. DON'T LET US KEEP YOU FROM YOUR BIG DAY!
BYE, PAUL.

PIGTAILS. IF HE ONLY KNEW.

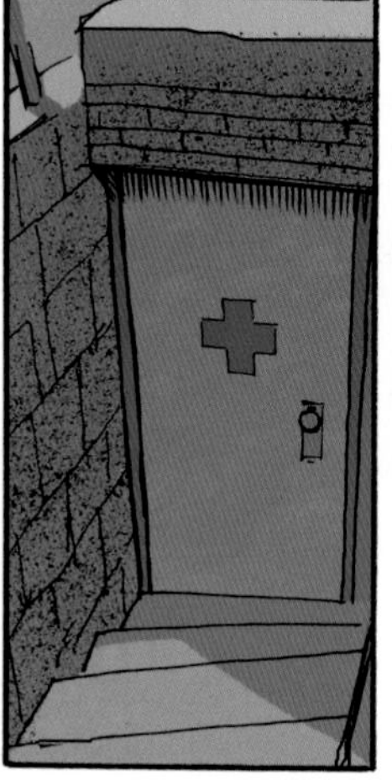

MAY I SPEAK FREELY?

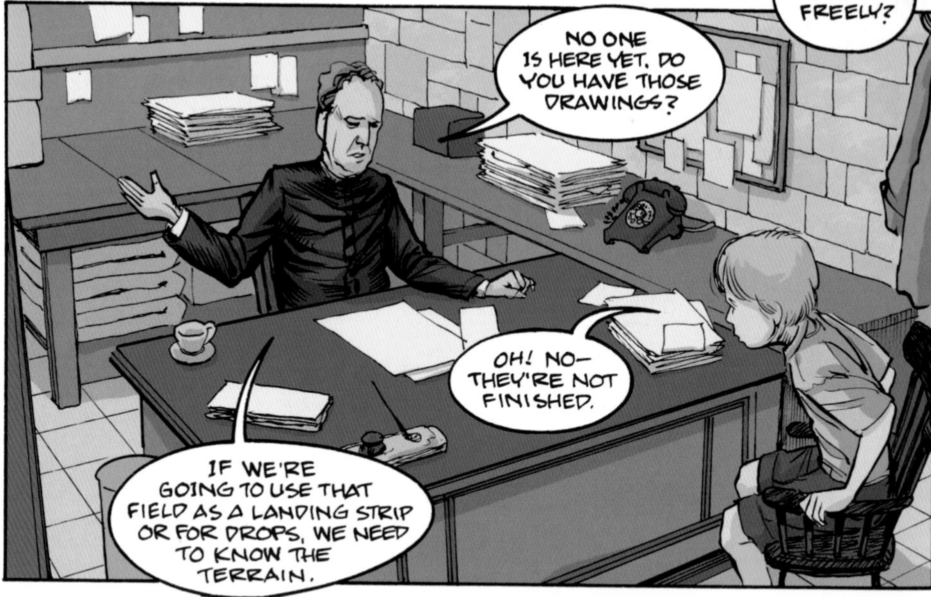
NO ONE IS HERE YET. DO YOU HAVE THOSE DRAWINGS?
OH! NO— THEY'RE NOT FINISHED.
IF WE'RE GOING TO USE THAT FIELD AS A LANDING STRIP OR FOR DROPS, WE NEED TO KNOW THE TERRAIN.

I CAN GO AGAIN TODAY.
MAKE A DETAILED SKETCH OF THE APPROACH FROM THE WOODS ON THE NORTH SIDE.
WHY?
... WAS THERE SOMETHING ELSE?

MY SISTER SYLVIE. SHE WANTS TO GET BACK IN THE GAME.
IS THAT WISE? JACQUES WAS CONCERNED ABOUT HER... DISCRETION.

JACQUES WANTED HER TO GATHER INTELLIGENCE. SHE SAID NO. THAT'S ALL.
BUT NOW SHE'S SAYING YES?
BECAUSE OF JACQUES. BECAUSE HE WAS SENT TO GERMANY. SHE WANTS TO HELP.

WHAT IS IT? HAS SOMETHING HAPPENED TO JACQUES?

JACQUES ISN'T IN GERMANY.

IS HE-

HE ESCAPED AND IS HIDING WITH THE **MAQUIS**, AS FAR AS I KNOW.

THAT'S GREAT! AND THAT'S WHAT HE WANTED MY SISTER'S HELP WITH. TO FIND OUT WHAT THE GERMANS KNOW ABOUT THE **MAQUIS**.

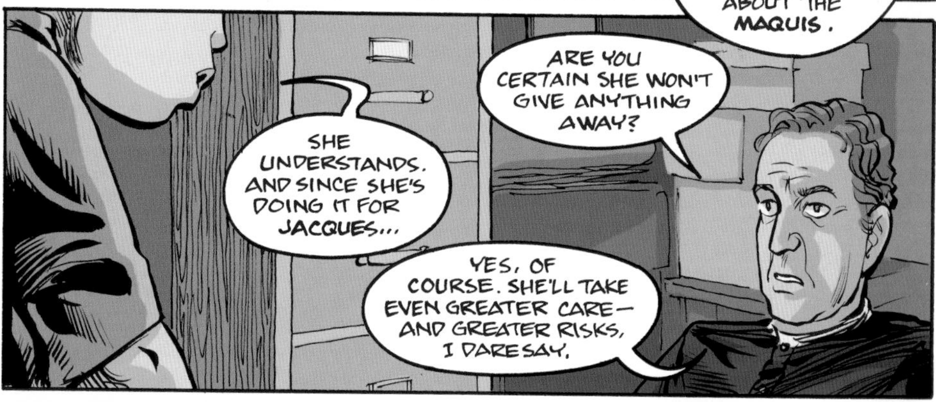
ARE YOU CERTAIN SHE WON'T GIVE ANYTHING AWAY?
SHE UNDERSTANDS. AND SINCE SHE'S DOING IT FOR **JACQUES**...
YES, OF COURSE. SHE'LL TAKE EVEN GREATER CARE— AND GREATER RISKS, I DARESAY.

HAVE YOU SEEN THE NEW BUTTERFLIES?
DEGAULLE'S SYMBOL. YES.
WHO DO YOU THINK IS POSTING THEM?

I THOUGHT IT WAS **YOU**.

IT COULD ALSO BE A TRICK. TO FIND OUT WHO IS A DEGAULLE SUPPORTER.

OH.

REMEMBER, YOU MUST TAKE CARE. THE MOST TRUSTWORTHY PERSON IN THE WORLD MAY BE KEEPING SECRETS.

DEADLY ONES.

AND SOMEONE YOU ASSUME IS YOUR ENEMY MAY VERY WELL SAVE YOU SOMEDAY. THESE ARE TURN-AROUND TIMES.

WONDERFUL.
THANK YOU FOR THE CLOTHING TICKETS.
WITH YOUR CHILDREN, YOU NEED THEM MORE THAN I DO. THAT SON OF YOURS SEEMS TO OUTGROW HIS TROUSERS DAILY!
I'M SURPRISED THEY'RE GROWING AT ALL, WITH ALL THE FOOD SHORTAGES.
I CAN'T REMEMBER THE TASTE OF REAL COFFEE ANYMORE.
AND STEAK. I SO LONG FOR A STEAK.
I DON'T KNOW HOW WE'LL SURVIVE.
WE WILL. WE HAVE TO.

SYLVIE! I HAVE SOMETHING TO TELL YOU!
SHOPPING IS A WASTE OF TIME, THERE'S NOTHING LEFT. I STOOD IN LINE FOR TWO HOURS!

COME ON!
WHAT'S WITH YOU?

I HAVE SOMETHING TO TELL YOU. SOMETHING YOU WANT TO HEAR.

JACQUES ISN'T IN GERMANY.
WHAT?

QUIT IT! WE DON'T WANT TO ATTRACT ATTENTION.

WONDER
WHERE ALL YOUR
FOOD IS GOING?
YOU THERE!

NO. I CAN'T RISK LEADING THEM BACK HOME.
NORTH SIDE OF FIELD, THE WOODS.
THE MAQUIS.

THAT BROTHER OF YOURS. DO YOU KNOW WHERE HE IS?
NO.
NO.
RUNNING WILD. GETTING UP TO GOD KNOWS WHAT.
THINGS ARE GOING TO CHANGE AROUND HERE!
YOU TELL HIM THAT HE IS TO COME STRAIGHT HOME AFTER SCHOOL TODAY. WE'RE GOING TO START HAVING SOME RULES!

École

WHERE'S PAUL?
MAMAN IS REALLY MAD AT HIM.
PAUL WASN'T IN SCHOOL TODAY.
WHAT?

I CAN'T KEEP MENDING THIS DRESS.
IS PAUL HERE?
HAVEN'T SEEN HIM.
DID YOU SEE HIM COME HOME LAST NIGHT?
I DON'T KNOW... I WAS IN MY ROOM.
MAYBE IF I ADDED SOME APPLIQUÉS?
I DON'T THINK HE CAME HOME. NOT LAST NIGHT. NOT TODAY.

GIVE ME BACK MY BROTHER!
Was ist..?
Nimm sie weg!
WHERE IS HE? I KNOW YOU TOOK HIM!
Hör auf!
MARIE! STOP!

WHERE'S PAUL?
Mach, dass dieses Mädel wegkommt!
I'M SO SORRY.
MARIE, STOP NOW!
GIVE HIM BACK!
MAY I HELP?
YOU SPEAK FRENCH?
A LITTLE.
TELL HIM I'M SORRY. MY SISTER IS UPSET BECAUSE OUR BROTHER IS GONE.
AH.
HE'LL BE FINE. HE'S JUST WORKING IN GERMANY.
NO. HE'S TOO YOUNG FOR THE COMPULSORY LABOR PROGRAM.
WE DON'T KIDNAP CHILDREN.

I KNOW! IT'S JUST— SHE'S SO SCARED. WE'VE LOST...

IT'S ALL RIGHT. I HOPE HE COMES HOME SOON.

WHAT'S YOUR NAME?
ERICH.

THANK YOU, ERICH.

ARE YOU CRAZY? STARTING A FIGHT WITH A GERMAN SOLDIER?

I CAN'T BELIEVE YOU WERE FLIRTING WITH HIM!

YOU'RE AS BAD AS AUNT CELIA!
LOWER YOUR VOICE!

DON'T YOU SEE? I CAN GET INFORMATION FROM HIM.

YOU'RE BRILLIANT!

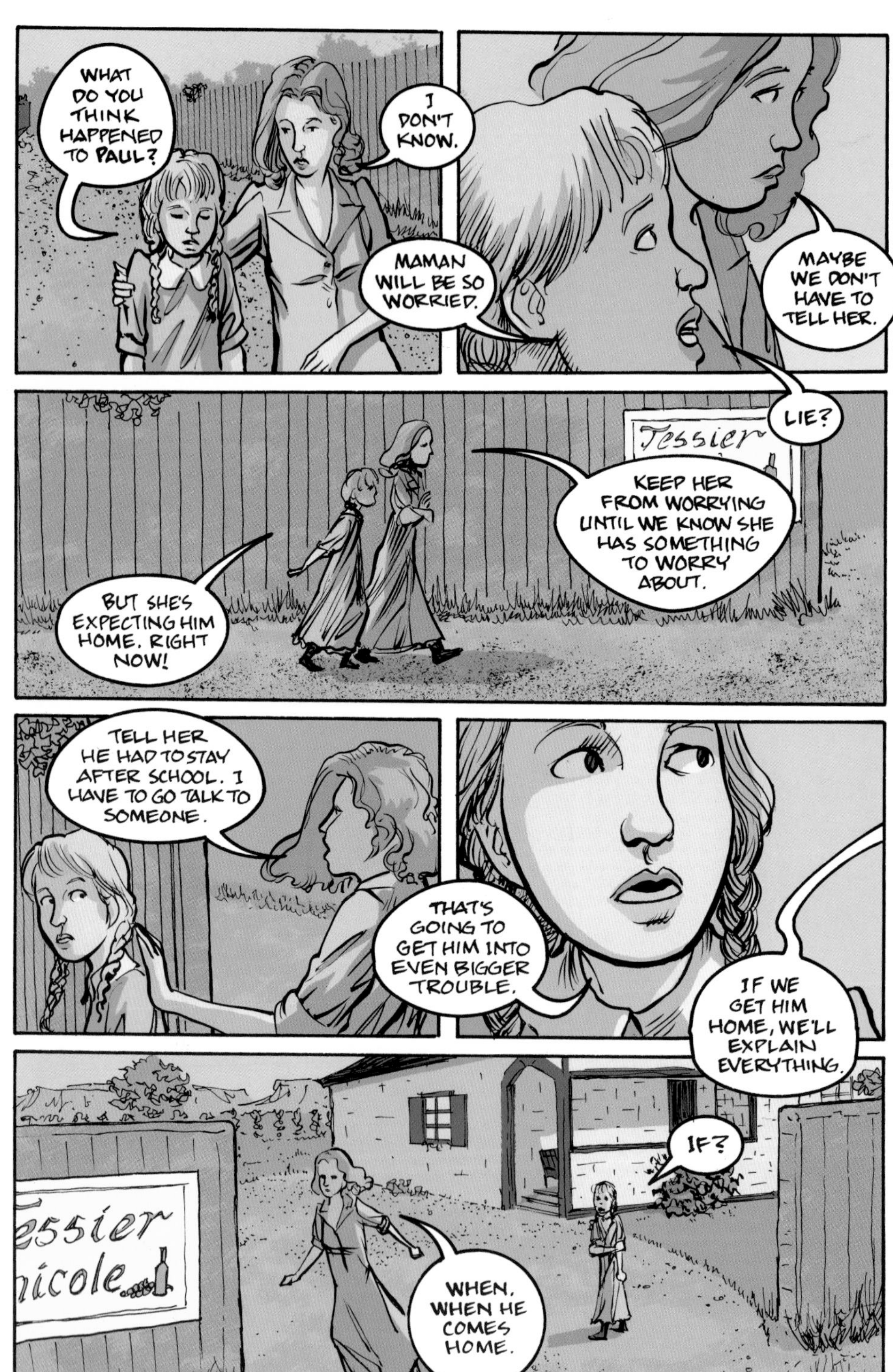
WHAT DO YOU THINK HAPPENED TO PAUL?
I DON'T KNOW.
MAMAN WILL BE SO WORRIED.
MAYBE WE DON'T HAVE TO TELL HER.
LIE?
KEEP HER FROM WORRYING UNTIL WE KNOW SHE HAS SOMETHING TO WORRY ABOUT.
BUT SHE'S EXPECTING HIM HOME. RIGHT NOW!
Tessier
TELL HER HE HAD TO STAY AFTER SCHOOL. I HAVE TO GO TALK TO SOMEONE.
THAT'S GOING TO GET HIM INTO EVEN BIGGER TROUBLE.
IF WE GET HIM HOME, WE'LL EXPLAIN EVERYTHING.
IF?
WHEN. WHEN HE COMES HOME.
essier
nicole

MISS TESSIER.
COME TO SEEK SOME OF THE LORD'S INTERVENTION ON YOUR BROTHER'S BEHALF?
EXCUSE ME?
I THINK YOU'LL DISCOVER THAT THERE ARE THOSE WHO LOOK OUT FOR BOYS SUCH AS PAUL.

PAUL IS MISSING.
I'VE HEARD.
HAS HE BEEN ARRESTED?

PLEASE. YOU MUST TELL ME WHAT YOU KNOW.

I BELIEVE HE HAS JOINED A GROUP IN THE MOUNTAINS.
THE MAQUIS?

BUT WHY WOULD HE DO THAT? WITHOUT TELLING ANYONE?
I FEAR FOR HIM. IF HE IS CAUGHT WITH THE MAQUIS HIS YOUTH WILL NOT HELP HIM.
WE HAVE TO MAKE HIM COME HOME!
YOU WOULD HAVE TO FIND HIM FIRST, AND THAT WOULD NOT BE EASY. AND HE MIGHT NOT WANT TO COME HOME.
MOST OF THE RÉSISTANTS WHO JOIN THEM ARE QUITE DEDICATED.
ONE MAY NOT AGREE WITH THEIR PHILOSOPHY, BUT YOU MUST ADMIRE THEIR PASSION.

ME AND MY BRIGHT IDEAS.
CRAK
CRAK
SPLOOSH
HEY! OVER HERE!
DON'T MAKE A MOVE.

PLEASE! I JUST—
WHO SENT YOU?
NO ONE! I-I WAS HIDING FROM THE MILICE.
WHY WOULD THEY BE AFTER YOU?
ANSWER ME!
HE'S RIGHT OVER HERE.
JEAN-PIERE HAS HIM!
HE JUST SNUCK UP ON US.

PAUL!
DON'T LET HIM SHOOT ME!
I DON'T THINK THAT'S GOING TO BE A PROBLEM.

IT'S ALL RIGHT. I KNOW THIS ONE.

HOW DID YOU FIND US?
LECLERC ASKED ME TO DRAW AN APPROACH TO THE FIELD FROM THE NORTH. I THOUGHT THAT MIGHT BE WHERE YOU'D BE HIDING.
CLEVER DEDUCTION.
BUT I GOT HOPELESSLY LOST.
YOU'RE LUCKY WE DIDN'T SHOOT YOU.
OH, RIGHT.

I THOUGHT THERE WOULD BE MORE OF YOU.
THERE ARE, JUST SCATTERED.
IT'S SAFER THIS WAY, HARDER TO FIND US.

AND IF THEY DO FIND US, FEWER ARRESTS, FEWER COMPROMISED AGENTS.

FEWER NAMES TO NAME IF WE'RE TORTURED.
WHAT WOULD YOU DO IF YOU WE'RE TORTURED? WOULD YOU TALK?

HE'D PROBABLY DO BETTER THAN YOU TWO.

HE SNUCK UP ON YOU. WHAT IF HE'D BEEN A NAZI? OR MILICE?

OR A COLLABORATOR?
HOW DO WE KNOW HE'S NOT?

BECAUSE I VOUCH FOR HIM.

HAVE YOU USED WEAPONS?
NO, SIR.

WE'LL START YOU THERE. SYLVESTER WILL SHOW THE OTHERS HOW TO MAKE EXPLOSIVES.
YEAH, I'LL GET HIM FIRING A BROOM HANDLE LIKE AN EXPERT.
IT'S A BEGINNING.

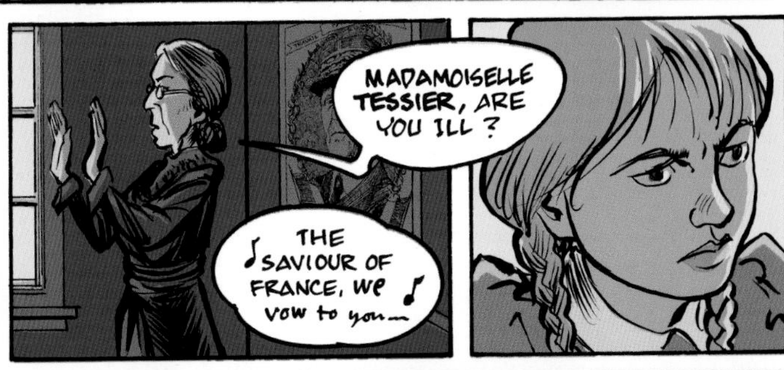

WHY AREN'T YOU JOINING US?

BECAUSE I DON'T WANT TO.

THERE WILL BE NO DISRESPECT IN THIS CLASSROOM. TO ME OR TO MARSHAL PÉTAIN.

THAT'S IT. TO THE PRINCIPAL WITH YOU.

I WON'T SING TO STUPID MARSHAL PÉTAIN FOR HIM EITHER.

OUT. NOW.

WE SHOULD SAY GOODNIGHT HERE.
YOU DON'T WANT ME TO WALK YOU ALL THE WAY HOME?
MY MOTHER... SHE WOULD BE... SHE WOULDN'T LIKE IT.
I SEE. I'M SORRY. I DON'T WANT TO CAUSE YOU TROUBLE. PERHAPS WE SHOULD NOT SEE EACH OTHER AGAIN.
NO!
THAT IS, NO, THAT WON'T BE NECESSARY.

IT'S GOING TO YOUR HOUSE.
IT'S PROBABLY MY AUNT CELIA. SHE HAS GERMAN... FRIENDS.
AH.
I SHOULD GO.
AS YOU WISH. WILL I- CAN I SEE YOU AGAIN?
OF COURSE.
SYLVIE.

YES, AUNT CELIA.
YOUR YOUNG MAN.
HE'S NOT MY YOUNG MAN.
THERE'S NOTHING TO BE EMBARRASSED ABOUT. HE'S QUITE GOOD LOOKING.
PLEASE DON'T TELL MAMAN. SHE'D BE FURIOUS.
YES, IT WOULD BE BEST IF WE KEPT IT JUST BETWEEN US. SHE HAS ENOUGH ON HER MIND.
THANK YOU.
HE SEEMS NICE.
YES. YES, HE IS.

PAUL ISN'T WITH YOU?
I'M SURE HE'S JUST OUT SOMEWHERE CAUSING TROUBLE. FATHERLESS BOYS HAVE SUCH—
HE HAS A FATHER!
THAT'S NOT WHAT I MEANT. GOOD LORD, YOU'RE SO TOUCHY ALL THE TIME.
THIS DISGUSTING CHICKORY. HOW ANYONE COULD THINK IT WAS COFFEE...
MAMAN, WILL YOU HELP ME HEM MY GREEN DRESS?
DID YOU HAVE A NICE TIME WITH GENEVIEVE?
YES. WE'RE GOING TO GET TOGETHER AGAIN TOMORROW.

I KNOW IT'S HARD FOR YOU TO KEEP REMAKING YOUR DRESSES...
MAMAN.
PAUL WON'T BE COMING HOME.
AT LEAST NOT FOR A WHILE.
TELL ME.
WE'RE PRETTY SURE HE'S JOINED ONE OF THE MAQUIS GROUPS.
HOW DO YOU KNOW THIS?
I THOUGHT YOU WEREN'T DOING ANY MORE RESISTANCE WORK!
PLEASE, MAMAN. YOU KNOW HOW IMPORTANT THIS IS.
I KNOW THAT I WANT MY CHILDREN ALL ALIVE WHEN THEIR FATHER COMES HOME.

I JUST WANTED YOU TO KNOW—SO YOU WOULDN'T WORRY.
THIS NEWS IS SUPPOSED TO KEEP ME FROM WORRYING? **MARIE** HAS BEEN SUSPENDED FROM SCHOOL, **PAUL** IS MISSING, AND YOU—

I'M NOT EVEN GOING TO THINK ABOUT WHAT YOU MIGHT BE UP TO.

WHAT ABOUT YOU? YOU WERE WORKING WITH **PASTOR LE CLERC** LONG BEFORE WE EVER DID ANYTHING!

I'M AN ADULT!

WHICH PUTS YOU AT MUCH MORE RISK.
WAR CHANGES PEOPLE. AND SOMETIMES IN WAYS THAT MAKE A MOTHER PROUD.

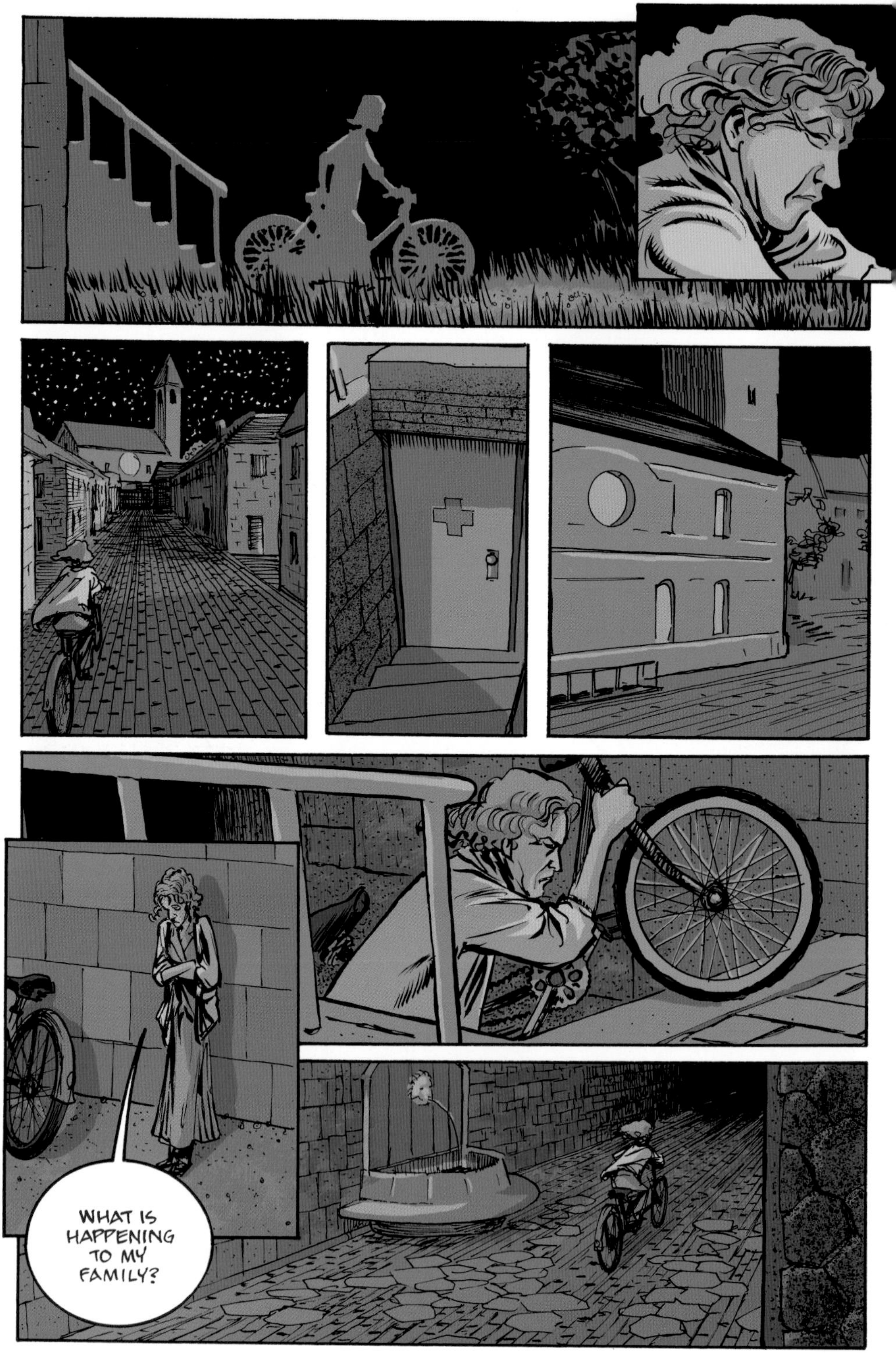

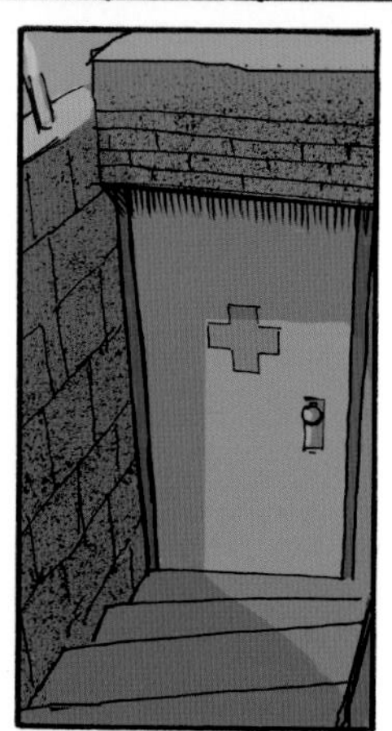

WHAT IS
HAPPENING
TO MY
FAMILY?

LIKE THIS?
THIS IS RIDICULOUS. WE'RE NOT GOING TO **SWEEP** THE GERMANS OUT OF THE COUNTRY.
WHY AREN'T WE USING REAL GUNS?
IF I WAS RUNNING THINGS, WE WOULD BE.
THERE'S GOING TO BE A SUPPLY DROP SOON, RIGHT? THAT WAS WHY I WAS SUPPOSED TO DRAW THE FIELD.
NOT SOON ENOUGH. AND THERE WON'T BE ENOUGH FOR EVERYONE.
WHICH IS WHY...

WHERE'D YOU GET IT?

I'LL BE READY.
EVER FIRED A WEAPON?
NO.
AIM AND SAY 'SHOOT' WHEN YOU PRETEND TO SQUEEZE THE TRIGGER.
SHOOT.

WHAT DID YOU DO THAT FOR?

THAT'S RECOIL. YOU HAVE TO BE PREPARED FOR IT.
OH.

I'VE SEEN GUYS A LOT BIGGER THAN YOU KNOCKED ON THEIR BACKSIDES BECAUSE THEY'D NEVER FELT RECOIL BEFORE. NOT GOOD WHEN SOMEONE IS SHOOTING AT YOU.

ARE THERE REALLY MORE OF YOU? US?
OH, YES. AND MORE ARE JOINING EVERY DAY.

WILL THERE BE FOOD IN THE DROP?

IF ALL GOES WELL, WE'LL KNOW SOON ENOUGH.
GETTING THE PACKAGES AFTER THE PLANES HAVE DROPPED THEM IS RISKY.
WHY?

TRAITORS. INTERCEPTED MESSAGES.
AND YOU CAN HEAR THE PLANES.
BUT AS LONG AS THE GERMANS AREN'T THERE WAITING FOR US, WE CAN USUALLY GRAB OUR SUPPLIES AND GET OUT OF THERE IN TIME.

THERE'S REAL MEAT IN THIS STEW! AND THE BREAD!
mmmmmmm!
IT IS GOOD HERE, YES?
OH, YES.

IS SOMETHING WRONG? YOU'VE BEEN VERY-
SORRY.
SORRY. YES. I MEAN, NO. NOTHING IS WRONG.
THEN WHAT IS IT?

I AM GOING ON A RAID VERY SOON. MY FIRST!
HOW EXCITING!
WHAT KIND OF RAID IS IT? A WAREHOUSE?
OH, NO. MUCH MORE IMPORTANT.
REALLY?
I GUESS YOU'RE NOT SUPPOSED TO TELL ME...
WELL, NO...

WE'RE GOING AFTER TERRORISTS IN THE WOODS.
WHAT'S WRONG?
ISN'T THAT DANGEROUS?
I'D HATE FOR ANYTHING TO HAPPEN TO YOU.
IT'S NICE FOR YOU TO CARE ABOUT ME.

HOW DO YOU KNOW WHERE THEY ARE?

I'VE BEEN IN THE WOODS ALL MY LIFE AND I **STILL** GET LOST.

WE HAVE VERY GOOD INTELLIGENCE THAT THE BRITISH WILL FLY IN SUPPLIES FOR THEM. WE HAVE UNCOVERED WHERE THEY PLAN TO DROP THE MATERIALS.

WHEN THESE TERRORISTS GO TO RETRIEVE THE ITEMS THEY WILL FIND US WAITING FOR THEM!

WHAT DO I DO? WHAT DO I DO?
YOU SCARED ME!
I WAS WEEDING. THE VINES DON'T LOOK VERY GOOD.
DID PAUL TELL YOU ANYTHING ABOUT WHERE THE MAQUIS WERE?
WHY? DID SOMETHING HAPPEN?
TELL ME! I CAN HELP!

ALL RIGHT. BUT I DON'T WANT MAMAN TO KNOW. SHE HAS TOO MUCH TO WORRY ABOUT.
I'M NOT A BABY!
THAT GERMAN BOY. HE TOLD ME THEY'RE GOING TO TRAP THE MAQUIS.
WE HAVE TO WARN THEM!
BUT I DON'T KNOW HOW TO FIND THEM.
PAUL'S DRAWINGS!

I THINK THIS IS HIS NEWEST ONE.

HE'S DRAWN THIS SAME FIELD SEVERAL TIMES. IT'S VERY DETAILED.

HE SOMETIMES DRAWS THINGS SO THE RESISTANCE CAN MAKE PLANS.

THIS PATH INTO THE WOODS IS MARKED ON ALL THE PAGES.
DO YOU THINK THAT'S WHERE PAUL WENT?

I THINK IT'S OUR ONLY CLUE. WE HAVE TO TAKE IT. AT DAWN.

I CAN'T WALK ANYMORE.
IT WILL BE DARK SOON. ALMOST TIME FOR THE DROP.
THIS IS CRAZY. WE'VE BEEN AT THIS ALL DAY. WE'RE NEVER GOING TO FIND ANYTHING.
BUT THE GERMANS WILL KILL THEM!
I NEED TO REST. THINK.
WE'LL FIND THEM AT THE FIELD. STOP THEM BEFORE THEY SIGNAL THE PLANE.
BUT THAT'S WHERE THE GERMANS ARE WAITING!
LET'S HOPE WE FIND THE MAQUIS FIRST.

WILL WE GET IN TROUBLE FOR SKIPPING SCHOOL?
WHY DO YOU CARE? YOU'VE BEEN SUSPENDED.

OH, RIGHT.

I CAN HARDLY SEE.
THAT MEANS THE GERMANS CAN'T SEE EITHER. AND IF THEY USE FLASHLIGHTS, WE'LL KNOW WHERE THEY ARE.
THAT'S WHERE THE PLANE WILL DROP THE SUPPLIES.
WHICH MEANS PAUL IS SOMEWHERE NEAR HERE.

HOW BIG IS THIS STUPID FIELD?
MAMAN IS GOING TO BE SO MAD AT US!
BRRUMBBBRRRUUMMBBRUMM
THE PLANE!
BRUMMB
HE'S GOING TO SIGNAL!

DON'T MAKE A SOUND!
SYLVIE!
THEY KNOW! THE GERMANS ARE HERE!
DON'T TRUST HER! SHE'S A SPY!
THESE ARE MY SISTERS!
WE SAW THEM! THEY'RE ON THE OTHER SIDE OF THE FIELD!
DON'T SIGNAL THE PLANE!
WHY SHOULD WE BELIEVE YOU?

WARN THE OTHERS! QUICKLY!
WHAT ARE YOU DOING HERE?
I CAN'T BELIEVE WE'RE TAKING ORDERS FROM GIRLS! WE DON'T EVEN KNOW IF THIS IS TRUE! SHE COULD BE—
MY SISTER WOULDN'T LIE.
AND SHE WOULD NEVER CLIMB A MOUNTAIN IF SHE DIDN'T HAVE TO.
HOW DID YOU FIND THIS OUT?
I- I DID WHAT YOU ASKED.
SHE PRETENDED TO LIKE A GERMAN BOY. HE TOLD HER.
HE WAS TRYING TO IMPRESS ME.

I KNEW YOU COULD DO IT.

I JUST HOPE CHARLES GETS TO THE OTHERS IN TIME.

IF THEY SIGNAL, THE PLANE WILL DO THE DROP. I'D HATE THE BOCHE TO GET THEIR HANDS ON OUR SUPPLIES!

IF THEY SIGNAL, THEY'LL GIVE AWAY THEIR POSITIONS!

WE NEED TO GET OUT OF HERE. NOW.
BUT WHAT ABOUT—
NOW.

WE CAN'T WAIT HERE TO SEE WHAT HAPPENS. WE'LL GO BACK TO CAMP TO REMOVE ANY CLUES AND THEN SPLIT UP.

NOW YOU'LL COME HOME!
WON'T YOU?

BUT IT'S ALMOST MY BIRTHDAY! AND PAPA WON'T BE THERE. OR HENRI.

GO HOME.
WHY?

YOU ARE MORE USEFUL TO US IN TOWN. YOUR DRAWINGS, YOUR POSTERS—
THE POSTERS.
HAS ANYONE BEEN TO THE HOUSE ASKING ABOUT ME?
NO. WHY?
YOU SEE? THE **MILICE** DIDN'T IDENTIFY YOU. GO BACK. HELP US AS ONLY **YOU** CAN.
IF YOU REALLY THINK...

YOU ARE A TRUE RÉSISTANT.
THAT MEANS YOU DO WHAT SERVES BEST.

A FEW DAYS LATER ...
I'M GLAD YOUR BROTHER IS SAFE.
WE ARE TOO.
WHERE WAS HE? AND WHY WAS YOUR SISTER SO CERTAIN THE GERMANS HAD HIM?

OH - HE HAD A BIG FIGHT WITH OUR MOTHER. I GUESS HE THOUGHT HE'D BE A BIG MAN AND RUN OFF.

HE LEARNED QUICKLY THAT BEING ON YOUR OWN ISN'T VERY EASY, ESPECIALLY AT HIS AGE.

IT'S HARD TO BE AWAY FROM HOME AT ANY AGE.
WHAT IS IT?

MAYBE YOU HAD THE WRONG PLACE?

MAYBE...

I'M JUST GLAD THAT YOU'RE ALL RIGHT.

THERE WILL BE ANOTHER OPPORTUNITY.

IT SMELLS DELICIOUS IN HERE!
IT'S AMAZING WHAT YOU CAN DO WITH THE RIGHT INGREDIENTS.

CAN I COME IN YET?
ENTER, BIRTHDAY GIRL.
REAL FOOD!

PORK CHOPS! BUTTERED POTATOES! AND A CAKE!
ALL YOUR FAVORITES.
IT LOOKS BEAUTIFUL.

WHERE DID-
HOW...?

SIT! BEFORE THINGS GET COLD!

I FORGOT TO TELL YOU!
YOU CAN'T CALL ME TEACHER'S PET ANYMORE.
WHY'S THAT?

BECAUSE I GOT THROWN OUT OF SCHOOL!

MARIE! THAT'S NOT SOMETHING TO BRAG ABOUT.

YOU DIDN'T GET THROWN OUT. YOU WERE SUSPENDED, TEMPORARILY.
I DON'T BELIEVE IT!

AND YOU'RE GOING BACK NEXT WEEK.
I WON'T SING THAT SONG! NOT EVER AGAIN!

I HAVE SOMETHING EXTRA SPECIAL FOR **MARIE**. I WAS GOING TO WAIT, BUT I THINK...

FROM PAPA?

YES.

Mlle. Marie Tessier
Tessier Vinicole
Jura, France
AREN'T YOU GOING TO OPEN IT?
I DON'T WANT TO RIP IT.
DO YOU WANT ME TO HELP YOU OPEN IT?
I'LL OPEN IT LATER.
MARIE, DON'T BE SILLY.
IT'S MARIE'S LETTER. SHE CAN DO WHATEVER SHE WANTS WITH IT.
CAN I HAVE MY **CAKE** NOW?

IS IT REAL CAKE? WITH REAL FLOUR?
YES, PAUL, IT IS. BUT YOU DON'T HAVE TO HAVE ANY IF YOU DON'T WANT IT.
YOU ARE A RUDE YOUNG MAN.
YOU'RE DOING THE RIGHT THING. FOR THE CHILDREN. FOR YOUR FAMILY.
AM I?

EVERYONE HAS TO BE NICE! IT'S MY BIRTHDAY!
EXACTLY SO. THIS IS **MARIE'S** SPECIAL DAY. **NOTHING** WILL SPOIL IT.
FOR THIS SPECIAL OCCASION WE'LL ALL DRINK A TOAST TO THE BIRTHDAY GIRL.
FLOUR
SUGAR
TO **MARIE**. OUR BIRTHDAY GIRL.
TO **MARIE**!

TO PAPA.
TO PAPA.
Mlle Maria Tessier
Tessier Vinicole
Jura, France
COME HOME SOON, COME HOME SOON.
SOON.
SOON.
SOON.

—Author's Note—

June, 1940: A French general is stripped of his rank. He is found guilty of desertion and treason.

August, 1944: A French general strides through the battle-scarred city of Paris. He arrives as a symbol of liberation, a savior, and the head of the new French government. He is cheered by thousands.

> These two men are the same man: General Charles de Gaulle.
> What a difference a war makes.

Even before the war began, de Gaulle was worried about the strength and skill of the French army. After serving with honor in WWI, he wrote books and articles criticizing the French army. His ideas angered many in the military—but he turned out to be right.

Because the French army used many tactics that de Gaulle had criticized, the German army was able to defeat the French so quickly it was known as a Blitzkrieg or "lightning war." De Gaulle was furious about France's surrender. He tried to convince the government to continue to fight. His arguments failed.

He continued the war against the Nazis anyway—in exile. He escaped to England, hoping to find a way to keep fighting. The day after Marshal Pétain announced the ceasefire (and the beginning of the Occupation), De Gaulle went on the radio from London. He urged the French people to resist. He couldn't face the Nazis in direct combat anymore, but he was still determined to save his country.

It wasn't easy. He was trying to fight a war an ocean away. He created the Free French Forces, a highly trained network of people operating under his orders in France, and worked with the British and Americans.

There were also well-organized, committed, and effective groups who weren't part of de Gaulle's Free French Forces. They didn't view de Gaulle as their leader and resented his dismissive attitude toward them. They were angry that he wouldn't provide them with supplies, but they also didn't think he should be giving them orders. After all, they were the ones actually doing the fighting in France. *He* was far away. *They* were the ones putting their lives on the line.

De Gaulle's personality didn't always help. He could be cold, haughty, and something of a snob. Everyone who knew him could see his powerful ambition, even his strongest supporters. Some people wondered which mattered more to him: the future of France or the future of de Gaulle.

In 1943 there was a surge of new recruits into the Resistance movement. That was the year the Nazis began sending French citizens to Germany, forcing them to work for the Nazi war effort. Young men and women went into hiding and found ways to fight back. De Gaulle finally acknowledged the power and importance of the different Resistance groups in France. They began to try to work together.

There were those in the Resistance and among the Allies who hated de Gaulle, mistrusted him, fought against him militarily and politically. There were also those who nearly worshipped him. But all would probably agree that there might not be a Paris today without him and all he did to *resist.*